A nail, a stick and a lid

Geraldine Kaye

Illustrated by Linda Birch

CHILDRENS PRESS, CHICAGO

Library of Congress Cataloging in Publication Data

Kaye, Geraldine.
  A nail, a stick, and a lid.

  SUMMARY: A little boy rescues his mother's cast-
off shopping bag and collects many useful things.
  [1. Collectors and collecting—Fiction]
I. Birch, Linda. II. Title.
PZ7.K212Nai3   [E]   75-40345
ISBN 0-516-03587-8

American edition published 1976 by
Regensteiner Publishing Enterprises, Inc.
All rights reserved. Printed in the U.S.A.
Published simultaneously in Canada.
First published 1975 by Knight books and
Brockhampton Press Ltd, Salisbury Road, Leicester
Printed in Great Britain by Cox & Wyman Ltd,
London, Fakenham and Reading
Text copyright © 1975 Geraldine Kaye
Illustrations copyright © 1975 Brockhampton Press Ltd

1932586

It was Saturday and Billy's Mom was
going shopping. She said, "I'm going to
get a new, cloth shopping bag today."

"May I have the old shopping bag?"
Billy said.

"It's got a hole in it," said June. "Silly
Billy."

Billy thought a bit. Then he got a pin
and fixed the hole. Billy was good at fixing
things. Billy went out with his bag.

"Got your pocket
money?" John said.

"Yes," said Billy.
"Getting candy?" said
Mike.

"No," said Billy. "I'm
getting something for my
bag."

Billy went down High
Street. He went to the tool
shop. There were silver
hammers in the window.

Billy went in. "I've got five cents" Billy
said. "What can I buy?"

"You can buy a few nails," the man said.

The man shook the nails out. They looked
like little silver fish.

Billy put the nails in his bag. He walked
down High Street. He saw lollipop sticks
and round tin lids like silver moons. Billy
picked up the tin lids and put them in his
bag.

Billy came to the park. There were lots of children on the swings. Billy walked under the trees and picked up sticks. He put them in his bag.

"What's in your bag, Billy?" Mike said.
"Moons and things," Billy said.
"Billy's silly," said John.

Billy sat and thought a bit. He took a
nail. He fixed a tin lid to a stick. Billy was
good at making things.

Billy pushed the stick along the ground.
The lid went around and around.

"What's that?" said Mike.

"It's a car," said Billy.

1932586

"We can make cars, too," said Mike.
"Yes," said John. "Let's get sticks
and lids."

But all the lids and sticks were in Billy's bag. Billy sat on his bag.

"Give us a lid, Billy?" Mike said.

"Give us a stick, Billy?" John said.

"Lids are a penny," said Billy.

"A penny just for an old lid?" said Mike.

"A penny for a lid and a stick and a nail," said Billy.

"All right," said John. "Here's a penny."

Billy gave John a lid and a stick and a nail.

"All right then," said Mike.

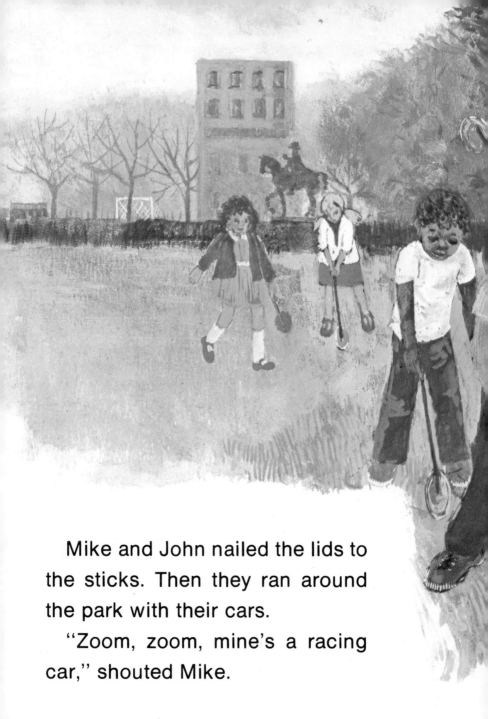

Mike and John nailed the lids to the sticks. Then they ran around the park with their cars.

"Zoom, zoom, mine's a racing car," shouted Mike.

All the boys wanted cars.

All the boys bought lids
and sticks and nails for a
penny.

They said, "Billy's not
silly."

The boys ran around and around the park.

"Zoom, zoom," they shouted. "I've got a racing car. Race you, Billy?"

June came to the park. "What's in your bag, Billy?"

"Twelve pennies," said Billy. "Would you like a lollipop?"

"Green," said June.

"I like red," said Billy.

Billy bought the lollies. Then he walked
along High Street with his car. "Zoom,
zoom," said Billy all the way home.